To all the children who have

never had a Christmas...

This book
belongs to...

CHARLIE

the

CHIMNEYSWEEP

and SOOTY

Written & Illustrated by
Bruce Peardon

Published by the Association of Mouth & Foot Painting Artists
©
ISBN No. 0 907159 41 9

Once there was a young boy named Charlie who worked as a chimneysweep. It was a very hard and dirty job to keep the chimneys clean so that the fires that warmed people's homes would burn nice and bright. Sweeps have to be small so that they can crawl into the fireplaces and clean away all the soot and ash; but Charlie did not mind the hard work, for chimneysweeps are said to be lucky people and Charlie had many friends.

Whenever he walked down the street carrying his brushes and brooms people would come up to him and touch him for luck, or they would call out to him:

"When can you come and clean my chimney, Charlie?"

And he would answer, "Maybe next week, for I have lots of work to do."

With so many friends he was always kept busy.

Charlie did not have a proper home for he was an orphan and he lived with his cat Sooty in the store-room of Mr Tibbs's bakery. In return for living in Mr Tibbs's bakery, Charlie swept the floors and cleaned the ovens and the chimneys in the bakery. Sooty's job was to catch the mice that tried to get into Mr Tibbs's bags of flour.

Mr Tibbs was a jolly man who always had a big smile and whenever he had a pie or a cake left over from his shop he would give it to Charlie for his dinner.

Charlie was always so busy he did not have any time to play, he had to get up very early each morning to clean the ovens for the day's baking and then off to work to sweep the chimneys. Sometimes, when he had to work in the big houses on the other side of town, he would stop for a few minutes on the way and watch the children skating on the lake in the park.

'Oh,' he thought, 'how I would love to stop and skate for a while. . . .'

But there was always so much work to be done; besides, skates cost a lot of money and as Charlie received only one penny for every chimney he swept, the money he earned had to buy new brushes and warm clothes.

So he had to be content to watch the
other children skate, while he dreamed that
one day he would be out there with them, on
his very own skates.

One day while Charlie was watching the children skating, a little girl broke away from the other skaters and came over to where he stood.

"Hello," she said cheerily, "what's your name?"

"Charlie", he replied, "what's yours?"

"Rebecca," she answered, "but my friends call me Becky. I've seen you down here at the lake often. You're a chimney-sweep aren't you? … Do you mind if I touch you for luck?"

Smiling, she reached out and touched his sleeve.

"Why don't you come skating? My friends would love to meet you."

"Well Becky," he said shyly, "I have to do some work and I don't have any skates."

"You can try mine," she said "they should buckle on to your boots, besides, I need a rest, I've been skating all morning."

"Are you sure you don't mind?" Charlie asked gleefully.

"Of course not," she replied as she began to undo the buckles on her boots.

Just as Charlie was about to tie on the skates a stern-faced woman came up to them.

"Come along Rebecca. I've told you before, do not speak to strangers and you must not lend your skates!"

" . . . But mother," Becky started to protest.

"No excuses my girl," her mother snapped, "now hurry up, we are late for the dressmaker, furthermore young lady, I do not want you speaking to this scruffy young boy again!"

"I'm sorry Charlie," whispered Becky sadly, "Mother is not very well and she doesn't mean to be unkind. Do forgive her."

"That's alright," said Charlie meekly. But Becky's mother had taken her by the hand and started off before he could say any more. 'I hope I haven't caused any trouble' Charlie thought as he watched Becky and her mother walk away, 'but I certainly would love to have tried the skates.'

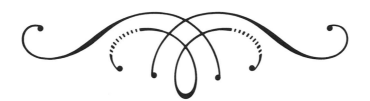

Christmas was drawing nearer and Charlie had to work even harder than before. Mr Tibbs had lots of orders for Christmas puddings and cakes, so Charlie had much more cleaning to do in the bakery. Many people wanted their chimneys swept for the cold winter nights so that the fires would burn brightly. Charlie was so busy he did not get a chance to watch the children skating but as he worked he wished that one day he could take Becky skating, with his very own skates.

Soon it was Christmas Eve and Charlie hung up his stocking over the big oven in the bakery.

"I don't want a lot of presents Father Christmas," Charlie said aloud, "but I really would love a pair of skates."

He gave Sooty a saucer of milk and hopped into his bed on top of the flour bags.

Snow was gently falling and the big clock in the town hall had just struck midnight when there was a tap on the window of the bakery storeroom. Charlie sat up, wide awake, to see a face with a big white flowing beard smiling at him through the window. It was Father Christmas himself!!

With a merry chuckle, the old man climbed through the window and sat on the end of Charlie's bed.

"I thought you came quietly and didn't let the boys and girls see you," stammered Charlie.

"Well," said Father Christmas, smiling, "that's what I normally do, but tonight I specially wanted to stop and talk to you, Charlie."

". . . But why?" asked Charlie excitedly.

Father Christmas stroked his beard and with a twinkle in his eyes, looked at the young boy and said:

"Well, my little man, once when it was Christmas and I delivered my gifts, my red suit would get very dirty from all the sooty chimneys I had to climb down. But since you have been the town sweep you have done such a good job keeping the chimneys clean, my suit looks as good as it was when I started my rounds, so I thought I would stop and thank you."

Charlie stared at Father Christmas, wide-eyed. "You came to thank me," he stammered.

"That's right," said the jolly old fellow, "and now I have a surprise for you. What is the present you would like most of all?"

"Well, Sir, if I wasn't asking too much," Charlie said shyly, "I would really love some skates . . ."

"Done," said Father Christmas with a roar of laughter, and he took from his toy sack the most beautiful pair of shiny skates Charlie had ever seen.

"Oh," cried Charlie "thank you so much Father Christmas, that's the most wonderful present I have ever had!"

"There is more," said Father Christmas and he handed the young boy a brightly wrapped package.

Excitedly Charlie opened it up to find a beautiful, warm vest and matching woollen cap that had a big pom-pom on top. There was also a new scarf and a new pair of trousers. Charlie was so delighted he was unable to speak. Sooty purred around Father Christmas's boots and the old man looked down and chuckled.

"I haven't forgotten you, my little friend," and he pulled a package from his sack. "There's a fish and a jar of cream for your Christmas dinner Sooty."

"I must go now, Charlie," said Father Christmas. "I have lots more toys to deliver.

Have a Merry Christmas and thank you for keeping the chimneys clean."

"Thank you," said Charlie. Then suddenly the jolly old man was out the window and had disappeared in a flurry of snowflakes. Charlie could still hardly believe his eyes even though the shiny skates were there beside the new clothes on his bed. "Oh Sooty" he said "what a beautiful present!"

And Sooty purred his agreement as he looked at the jar of cream and the fish Father Christmas had left him. "You can't have those now Sooty!" said Charlie as he picked up the package. "That's for your dinner tomorrow." So saying, he put the fish and the cream in the storeroom cupboard. "Now we must go back to sleep, for we have an exciting day ahead."

At first it was hard to go to sleep for Charlie kept thinking of his wonderful present, but soon he was sleeping soundly and dreaming of the fun he would have skating on the lake.

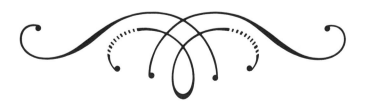

Charlie awoke early on Christmas morning to the lovely sound of the town church bells. He hopped out of bed and Sooty greeted him with a happy meow.

"Merry Christmas Sooty." Charlie replied.

Sooty gave another meow and looked longingly at the cupboard where the fish and cream were.

"All right," chuckled Charlie, "you can have them now. I don't suppose it will matter if you have a Christmas breakfast."

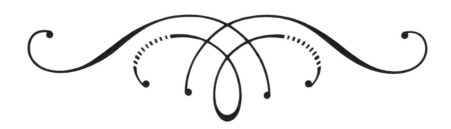

He gave the cat the present and then he filled a tub with warm water and got into it. As he bathed he sang all the carols he knew, so filled with joy was he on this wonderful Christmas morning.

After he had finished his bath, Charlie put on his new clothes, took his shining new skates and excitedly hurried off to the lake.

When he arrived, all the other children were there and sitting down buckling on her skates, was Becky. "Merry Christmas Becky" said Charlie as he came up beside her.

At first she didn't recognise him and then she said, "Oh it's you Charlie. Merry Christmas. I didn't know you in your new clothes . . . and you have some skates!" she said gleefully. "Now you can come out on the lake with me."

As Charlie buckled on his new skates he told Becky how he had met Father Christmas and when he had told the story, Becky said how happy she was for him. Soon the skates were firmly buckled on and he was ready for his first try.

"Take hold of my hand," said Becky, "for it may be a little difficult for you at first."

But Charlie was wobbly only for a short time and then he was skating as well as the other children.

Charlie and Becky did not notice the time pass by as they merrily skated. Then suddenly Becky heard her name being called. They both looked around and there was a man standing on the edge of the lake waving to her.

"Oh dear." said Becky, "It's my father. I promised I would be home early for dinner, but the time has gone so quickly while we were having fun."

"I hope your father will not be angry" said Charlie.

"No," smiled Becky as they moved toward her father, "he will understand. Father is a very kind man. My mother is a very kind and gentle person," she added, "she's not always short with people as she was when you first met her, Charlie. It's just that she gets upset sometimes … I think it is when she thinks of my little brother. You see, he died of the fever and mother misses him very much, so when she is sad she says things she does not mean."

"I understand," said Charlie softly.

"I have a wonderful idea," said Becky excitedly "Why don't you come and have Christmas dinner at my home Charlie? Then you could see for yourself that mother is a lovely person."

"I don't think so," he stammered, "I would not like to be a bother."

"Oh, please say you will, Charlie," she pleaded, "I will ask father, I am sure he will not mind."

They reached the place where Becky's father stood. "Hello Rebecca," he smiled. "I thought you may not have wanted your Christmas dinner." But Becky knew he was only making fun.

"Father, this is my friend, Charlie" she said, "could he come and share Christmas dinner with us ... you see, he has no family and no-one to share Christmas with because he lives in the bakery and ..."

"Hold on, young lady," chuckled Becky's father, "not so quickly. Now, tell me about it again, slowly."

Becky told her father again, and when she had finished, he smiled. "Of course you may come to dinner with us, Charlie, you are most welcome. Now come on you two rascals, or the turkey will be cold." Becky's father took them each by the hand and they hurried off home.

When they arrived, Charlie waited in the parlour while Becky ran off to change into her best dress and her father went to tell her mother Charlie would be staying for dinner.

Very shortly Becky's mother came into the parlour, Charlie could see she had tears in her eyes as she bent down and hugged him to her. "Welcome to our home, Charlie," she said softly, "and a very Merry Christmas … No little child should have to spend Christmas alone."

Then taking him by the hand with Becky and her father following, she led them into the most beautiful dining room Charlie had ever seen.

In one corner stood a brightly decorated Christmas tree and upon seeing it Charlie stammered, "I haven't brought a present ma'am, but I could come back tomorrow and clean your chimney for free."

"There's no need for you to worry about presents," said Becky's mother as she put her arm around his shoulders, "your smile is the best gift you could give us."

With that, they all sat at the table and Becky's father carved the turkey and they ate the most delicious food Charlie had ever tasted. There was much laughter as they ate and talked, and Becky thought her mother looked the happiest she had ever seen her.

When dinner was over they began to unwrap the presents from beneath the Christmas tree.

"You can share mine Charlie," said Becky excitedly, "help me open this big parcel!"

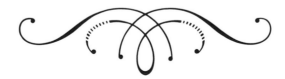

As they started to unwrap the gifts, Becky's parents slipped quietly from the room. They returned shortly and Becky's father went to Charlie and gently put his hand on the boy's head.

"Charlie, how would you like to come and live with us forever?" he said, "We would be very happy if you would. You could have your very own room and go to school with Becky. We would love to have a little boy in our home again."

Charlie was so delighted he could not speak.

Becky ran and hugged her mother. "Oh thank you mother," she cried, "I am so happy." Charlie finally got his voice back and said, "Can Sooty come to stay as well?"

"Of course he can. I think it would be nice to have a cat about the house," said Becky's father cheerily.

"I would still have to clean Mr Tibbs's bakery for him," added Charlie, "for he may not be able to get anyone to do it and he was very good to me when I had no-one."

"I think it is very good of you to think of Mr Tibbs," said Becky's father. "It is important that you are loyal to your friends."

"Thank you all very much," Charlie said "you have given me a lovely home."

Becky's mother kissed him and Charlie said, "Maybe it's true after all, chimney-sweeps are lucky!"

They all laughed merrily and outside the shadows grew longer as the moon peeked above the houses to signal the end of a wonderful Christmas day.

THE END

Bruce Peardon

Bruce Peardon was born in Brisbane, Queensland, Australia in 1945. While serving with The Royal Australian Navy he was seriously injured in a motor accident. The severe spinal damage resulted in total paralysis from his neck down.

Bruce had always been interested in art and naturally progressed to painting by holding the brush in his mouth. He mastered this unique skill and became a member of the Association of Mouth and Foot Painting Artists.

He continued to develop his skills, both in watercolour and oils, and his art is held in high esteem. His works hang in private and public collections in his own country and overseas.

Bruce gave tirelessly of his time and expertise to aspiring young artists who had lost the use of their arms. He worked hard for the advancement of the Association of Mouth and Foot Painting Artists.

Bruce died suddenly in May 2001. He is survived by his wife Chris and their son Ben. His death left a void in the lives of all who knew him. He will be remembered for his friendship, his belief in the youth of the world and his unbridled love of life.